THE TURTLE AND
HIS FOUR FRIENDS

Written By

Charity Nnamoko

EBOOK ISBN:978-627-7544-40-9

PRINT ISBN: 978-627-7544-41-6

THE
TURTLE AND
HIS FOUR FRIENDS

Written By

Charity Nnamoko

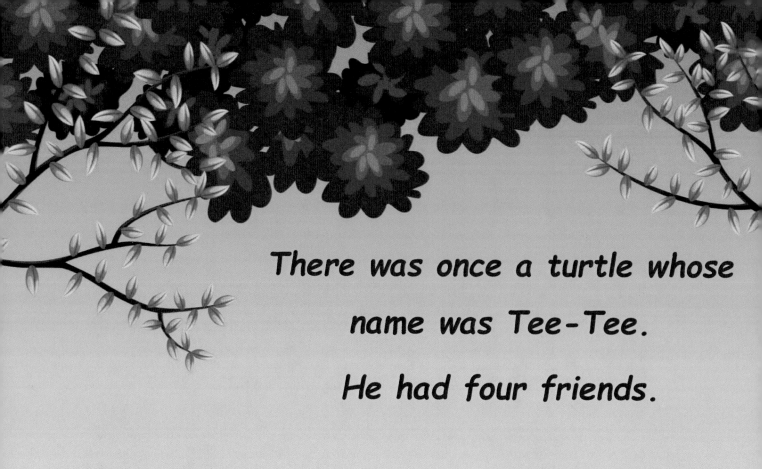

There was once a turtle whose name was Tee-Tee.
He had four friends.

His first friend was named Parrot.

His second friend was named Eagle.

His third friend was named Pigeon.

His fourth friend was named Peacock.

Tee-Tee was a very selfish turtle.
He only cared about himself.
He did not like to share things
with his friends, and he was very
tricky too.

Even though Tee-Tee was selfish, his
friends were kind.
They liked to help each other and
share what they had with Tee-Tee.

There was a king who lived on top of a tall mountain, King Owl. He liked to have parties and celebrate with friends.

One day the king decided to have a big party.
He invited Tee-Tee, Parrot, Eagle, Pigeon, and Peacock to the party.

Tee-Tee's friends were very happy to be attending a party held by the king. Tee-Tee was very sad because he thought he would not be going to the party with his friends.

"Why are you sad Tee-Tee?" Asked Eagle. Tee-Tee told his friends that he was unhappy because there was no way he could get to the top of the mountain in time to attend the party.

"I don't have wings and I can't fly as you all do," Tee-Tee said.

Tee-Tee's friends got together to think of a way to help their friend.

Eagle suggested donating half of his wings to Tee-Tee but

Pigeon reminded Eagle that he would not be able to fly with just one-half of his wings.

So, Tee-Tee's friends had to think of something else.

After a long time of thinking of different ways, they could help their friend Tee-Tee get to the top of the mountain for the party, Parrot had a great suggestion.

He suggested that since Eagle is big and can fly very high, he should give Tee-Tee a lift on his back to the top of the mountain.

Eagle, Pigeon, and Peacock agreed to what Parrot suggested.

They all went to find Tee-Tee. With excitement, the friends told Tee-Tee of their plan, and he was very happy that he would be able to attend the king's party.

The day finally came for Tee-Tee and his friends
to attend the party.
They decided to count down from five before they
took off.
So, the countdown began with Tee-Tee already
balanced on Eagle's back.
Five, four, three, two – before they got to number
one, Tee-Tee stopped them because he wanted to
say something before they took off.

Tee-Tee told his friends that he had decided to
change his name to "All of you". He told his
friends to call him by the new name when they
get to the party.
His friends agreed, and the countdown began
again. Five, four, three, two, and one.
All five friends flew to the top of the mountain
for the King's party.

When they arrived, the king welcomed
them with excitement.
Tee-Tee quickly told the king that his
new name is, "All of you."
The king smiled and went on to welcome
some of the other guests.

There were other animals already
at the party when Tee-Tee and
his friends arrived.

There were a lot of food and drinks at the party.

One of the king's servants brought food to the five friends.

Before the servant left the room, Tee-Tee, now called "All of you," asked the servant; "who are these for?" The servant answered, "for all of you."

Once the servant left the room, "All of you" turned to his four friends and said, "Did you hear what the servant just said?" He said the food is all mine because my name is "All of you".

His friends were sad and surprised but said nothing. They quietly watched "All of you" finish all the food and drink alone without sharing with his friends.

Tee-Tee's friends were angry with him for eating all the food and the drinks all by himself without sharing with them. They now realized why he changed his name before they came to the party. It was so he has all the food and drinks for himself.

Tee-Tee's friends thought of ways they could teach him a lesson. They agreed not to give him a ride back home.

They went to the king, thanked him for inviting them to the party, and flew back home leaving "All of you" behind.

After some time, the rest of the guests left except for "All of you." He sat down thinking of what to do and feeling bad for what he did to his friends.

When Tee-Tee saw that the sun was setting and that it was going to be dark soon, he decided to jump down from the high mountain.

He went to the edge of the mountain, closed his eyes, and counted from one to three, and jumped down from the mountain.

Ahhhhhhhhhhhhhhhhhhhhhh. CRASH!

When Tee-Tee jumped down, he landed on a rock and his shell broke into pieces. He lay down there crying for help. His friends' Parrot, Eagle, Pigeon, and Peacock heard Tee-Tee's voice and ran quickly to check if he was ok.

Tee-Tee told his friends that he was sorry for what he did at the party. He also asked them to forgive him for tricking them and changing his name to "All of you."

Tee-Tee"s friends forgave him and helped glue his broken shells back together

Tee-Tee's shell was fixed, but it was not smooth anymore. It had lines where the pieces of shell were glued together.

Tee-Tee made some promises to his friends. Firstly, he promised not to answer "All of you" anymore or change his name ever again. Secondly, he promised never to trick his friends again.
Thirdly, he promised to always share things with his friends.
And lastly, he promised to always be there for his friends and ready to help them any time.
Tee-Tee and his friends were all happy once again.

Dear parents, teachers, and caregivers,

This is an interactive storybook. I heard this story from my dad so many times as a child and it helped me learn how to be a good friend, how to share and relate well with people.

Feel free to as your child (ren) questions while you are reading to them and allow them time to respond and explain what they understand and what they could have done differently as Tee-Tee's friends or as Tee-Tee.

As an educator, this story can help you plan a lesson for your students on friendship or how to develop social skills.

Sample questions to ask the children at the end of the story.

- ❖ What do you think this picture portrays?
- ❖ Why is it that Tee-Tee does not like to share with his friends?
- ❖ Why did Tee-Tee change his name to "All of you"?
- ❖ Was Tee-Tee being a good friend by eating all the food meant for him and his friends?
- ❖ Why did Tee-Tee's friends leave the party without him?
- ❖ Did Tee-Tee learn to be a better friend through his experiences?
- ❖ Do you think that the shells of turtles look like many patches held together with glue?
- ❖ Do you think the Turtle's broken shell is the reason all turtles now have patched shells?